100% UNOFFICIAL

# BTS

**EVERYTHING YOU
NEED TO KNOW ABOUT
THE KINGS OF K-POP**

First published in Great Britain in 2020 by Dean,
an imprint of Egmont UK Limited,
2 Minster Court, 10th floor, London, EC3R 7BB
www.egmont.co.uk

Written by Malcolm Mackenzie
Designed by Ian Pollard

100% Unofficial: BTS copyright © Egmont UK Limited 2020

ISBN 978 1 4052 9743 1
70895/001
Printed in Italy

Egmont takes its responsibility to the planet and its inhabitants very
seriously. We aim to use papers from well-managed forests run by
responsible suppliers.

# BTS

## EVERYTHING YOU NEED TO KNOW ABOUT THE KINGS OF K-POP

Malcolm Mackenzie

# CONTENTS

# THE POWER OF 7

BTS are the biggest – and some would argue best – boy group in a generation. Proving that seven really is heaven.

**V**
... *also known as*
- Taehyung
- TaeTae

**SUGA**
... *also known as*
- Yoongi
- Agust D

**JIN**
... *also known as*
- Seokjin
- Worldwide handsome

The best boybands used to have five members, but how much better might Take That, Backstreet Boys and One Direction have been with two more members? In K-Pop seven is seen by many as the ideal number: just ask Got 7. In seven years, BTS have gone from rookies to the biggest pop group in the world! It's not hard to see why: catchy songs with unusually insightful lyrics that they write themselves, the most jaw-dropping music videos in which they kill insane choreography flawlessly, and wearing fashions most of us can only dream of. They are funny, friendly, warm and welcoming, handsome, humble and honest. They are BTS and their talent is bulletproof. We are ARMY and our devotion is unshakeable.

**JUNGKOOK**
*... also known as*
- JK
- Kookie
- Golden Maknae

**RM**
*... also known as*
- Namjoon
- Rap Monster

**JIMIN**
*... also known as*
- Mochi
- ChimChim
- Jiminie

**J-HOPE**
*... also known as*
- Hobi
- Hoseok

# TRAINEES TO ROOKIES

**There was a time when BTS were unknowns – jump in the time machine and explore those early days.**

Creating the perfect group is a job so tricky it almost verges on magic.

## MAKING THE BAND

BTS was conceived ten years ago by a small entertainment company, Big Hit, led by Bang Si-Hyuk – one of the founders of JYP, home of TWICE.

As a remarkably-talented young rapper gathering momentum in the underground scene of Seoul, RM was first to be recruited for the BTS project. Next was Suga, another emerging rapper and skilled producer.

J-Hope, with his incredible dance skills, soon followed – the fact he had rap skills was a bonus. With his striking good looks, Jin was spotted on the street – after all, every band needs a 'visual'. Jin had no experience before he was signed with Big Hit, but

**Big Hit big daddy: Bang Si-Hyuk**

with hard work he became the respected all-rounder he is today. Jungkook caused a 'bidding war' between entertainment companies after appearing on a TV talent show *Superstar K*. JK chose Big Hit over the other companies because he was so impressed with RM – phew!

When talent scouts came to Daegu, V had no intention of auditioning – he was only there to support a friend – but someone cleverly convinced him to try out. He made it through on raw talent and charisma. Last to join was Jimin, who was urged to audition by his dance teacher. Out of all of the BTS boys, Jimin's training time was the shortest.

# EARLY DAYS

BTS might be the biggest band on the planet now, but success was slowly won. When they released their first mini-album *2 Cool 4 Skool* on 12 June 2013, there was a buzz and the album got to number five in their homeland. However, their debut single *No More Dream* disappointingly only made it to number 124 in the Korean charts. Their next single *We Are Bulletproof Pt. 2* failed to chart at all. Three months later they released their follow-up EP and the single *N.O*, but it didn't fare much better. A battle lay ahead for the boys, but did they quit? No way! At the end of the year, things started looking up when BTS won some new artist awards and their third EP *Skool Love Affair* went to number one on the Gaon chart. It was early days, but Bangtan Boys were well on their way.

**V**

**SUGA**

**JIN**

Hip-hop heavy TV performances of *No More Dream* introduced seven unknowns that would soon take over the world.

**JUNG KOOK**

**RAP MONSTER**

**JIMIN**

**J-HOPE**

# STARDOM BECKONS

## Our heroes conquer South Korea with a softer sound, and stunning, thought-provoking visuals.

In 2016 BTS were suddenly standing out from the crowd – easy to see why.

## SINGLE SUCCESS

There was always an appetite for BTS, but their original hip hop and rock concept was holding them back from massive mainstream success. A shift began to take place in 2015 with the release of their third EP *The Most Beautiful Moment in Life: Part 1*. Its lead single *I Need U* was BTS's first big hit in Korea, debuting at number five on the Gaon Digital and Download charts and went on to win a number of music show awards. While follow-up *Dope* was not a mega smash, it did become the band's first song to reach 100 million

views on YouTube. The follow-up EP *The Most Beautiful Moment in Life: Part 2* built on the boys' success, yielding a top 10 hit on the Gaon chart with *Run*.

*Dope* was pretty darn dope.

# KINGS OF K-POP

2016 was the year BTS became huge at home – three years after their debut. With the release of their second studio album *Wings* and the single *Blood Sweat & Tears* they obliterated the K-Pop competition, rocketing to number one on nearly every chart and breaking records all over the place. The compelling video to *Blood Sweat & Tears* showcased a sensitive artistic vision, gaining over six million views in 24 hours – a record at that time for a K-Pop group. The album *Wings* sold 1.5 million copies in South Korea making it the most popular album of all time on the Gaon album chart. If that wasn't enough, BTS rounded out 2016 winning the covetted 'Artist of The Year' at the Mnet Asian Music Awards. With the Asia ARMY fully mobilised it was time for the rest of us to sit up and take notice.

The *Blood Sweat & Tears* MV was a visual feast.

Engaging performances made audiences desperate for more Bangtan Boys.

# WORLD DOMINATION

**Bangtan Boys go from K-Pop's hottest thing to the biggest, stadium-slaying, most watched band on earth.**

BTS are winning awards galore! Dusting them all must be a such chore.

## AMERICA'S ANGELS

From 2017 onwards, BTS's success was a runaway train – like the one depicted in the MV to *Spring Day*. Every release seemed to sell more, get more views, more likes. After a brand refresh BTS came back with *Love Yourself: Her* and it was a revelation. The EP broke into the top ten of the US Billboard chart and cracked the UK album chart, sandwiched between their heroes Eminem and Ed Sheeran at number 14. In their homeland, it became the biggest-selling album of all time, breaking their own record – something they would go on to do again and again. The lead single *DNA* became the most watched K-Pop video on YouTube in a 24-hour period. Fast forward a year and BTS are not just breaking K-Pop most-viewed YouTube records, they are beating the likes of Taylor Swift and Ariana Grande.

Literally making the world a more colourful place in the *DNA* MV.

# BIG HITTERS

By the time BTS released *Love Yourself: Tear* in 2018 they were a phenomenon the likes of which the world had never seen! Naturally the EP went straight to number one in America. It was no surprise that by this point the biggest artists in the world were queuing up to work with the boys. Nicki Minaj's appearance on mega-hit *Idol* made even the most sceptical sit up and pay attention. Collabs with Halsey, Charli XCX, Zara Larsson and Ed Sheeran followed, along with multiple appearances on international chat shows, endorsements with global corporations such as Coca Cola and

Nicki Minaj adds extra oomph to *Idol*.

Nike, a number one mobile app, a sold out stadium tour, record breaking concert film, and perhaps the most surprising: an appointment as ambassadors for the United Nations. Right now it's hard to imagine how the band can get any bigger!

Despite their unprecedented level of success BTS remain thankful.

# BEYOND THE SCENE

**What's in a name? Quite a lot actually. Korean pop music loves a double or even triple meaning.**

- The name BTS stands for Bangtan Sonyeodan in Korean, which translates as Bulletproof Boy Scouts, which stands for the boys' belief in fighting against the pressure (the bullets) that society puts on us to conform.

- J-Hope has explained that Bangtan means to guard against something, explaining that the band "will boldly defend our music and our value."

- In Japan the band are known as Bodan Shonendan.

- For the first four years of their career BTS was represented by a logo featuring a cool bulletproof vest.

- Some names considered before the band settled on Bangtan Sonyeodan were Big Kids and Young Nation. Fans all agree that BTS works much better.

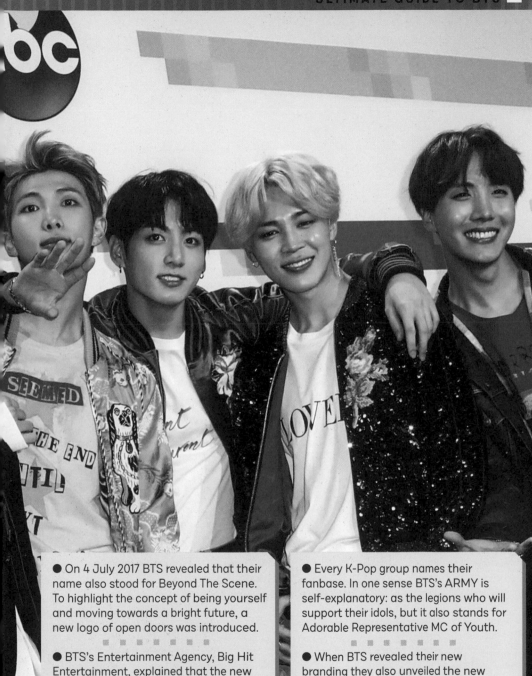

● On 4 July 2017 BTS revealed that their name also stood for Beyond The Scene. To highlight the concept of being yourself and moving towards a bright future, a new logo of open doors was introduced.

● BTS's Entertainment Agency, Big Hit Entertainment, explained that the new BTS logo "symbolises youth who don't settle for their current reality and instead open the door and go forward".

● Every K-Pop group names their fanbase. In one sense BTS's ARMY is self-explanatory: as the legions who will support their idols, but it also stands for Adorable Representative MC of Youth.

● When BTS revealed their new branding they also unveiled the new design for their fan base, ARMY, which represents the other side of the pair of doors of BTS's logo.

## 김남준

**Name:** Kim Nam-joon

**Born:** 12 September 1994

**Star sign:** Virgo (organised, critical, faithful)

**From:** Goyang, South Korea

**Height:** 5 feet 11 inches (the tallest member of BTS)

**Defining features:** An adorable dimple

**Usual position:** Third from right

# RM

## ARMY are so proud of RM, we wish he could lead us all – even if it's just round the aisles of Tesco.

### MONSTER X

RM stands for Rap Monster, which Namjoon clearly is. Before he settled on this moniker he was known as Runch Randa, but the best nickname he has is God of Destruction, because he's so clumsy that he breaks everything.

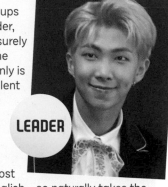

Most K-groups have a leader, and RM is surely amongst the best. Not only is he an excellent role model, talented songwriter and performer, he is the most fluent in English – so naturally takes the lead in all overseas media interactions.

**LEADER**

### PROBLEMATIC

Fans might argue whether Jin or V is the true visual of BTS, but RM has the hottest brain, or at least that's what the makers of the *Problematic Men* TV variety show think. RM was a regular star of the programme, discussing a series of modern conundrums.

### MR TUMBLE

It is well known that RM isn't naturally the best dancer, but sometimes even standing up is hard work for Namjoon. During a performance at the Mnet Asian Music Awards: Fans' Choice in Japan in December 2018 RM's astronaut inspired outfit got the better of him and he toppled onto his bum, much to the delight of his bandmates.

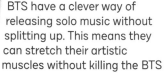

### MONO

BTS have a clever way of releasing solo music without splitting up. This means they can stretch their artistic muscles without killing the BTS dream. Fans and critics alike came out in support of RM's mixtape *Mono*.

# SONGS
## TO DOWNLOAD

**BTS have a wealth of top notch bops – let's dive into some of the best of them.**

### DANGER (2014)

This early single from BTS, their first from their first full length album *Dark and Wild*, is classic old-school Bulletproof Boy Scouts. A heavier sound than we've come to love, with wigged-out hip-hop loops, growls of electric guitar and football terrace chants. This song about a relationship in *danger* features a high-pitched hook from Jimin and some rapping from Jungkook.

**1**

### BOYZ WITH FUN (2015)

A throwback party anthem where the boys tell us repeatedly how much fun they are, as if we needed convincing. Soulful basslines, playful horns and a skittering snare drum all urge us to shake our tailfeathers. It's all a bit crazy with the boys having a conversation with each other but that all adds to the house party vibe. Basically, their *Uptown Funk*.

**2**

**3**

### I NEED U (2015)

A massive slow-build power ballad that starts with heavy sighs and finger snaps and crescendos into an explosive emo outpouring. *I Need U* is the beginning of BTS starting to sound like a world-conquering boyband, so perhaps it's no coincidence that The Beatles and Westlife both have songs called *I Need You*. This is very much pop with elements of hip hop.

## BLOOD SWEAT & TEARS (2016)

Even without the totally epic MV, this song is packed with drama making it a definite contender for Bangtan's greatest single. It soars and soars on evocative duck quacks and then comes crunching back to earth with J-Hope's pleading chorus. It sounds like he's asking for money, money but all he actually wants is his unrequited love to be returned. It's very emotional.

## FAKE LOVE (2018)

A more subtle single, *Fake Love* is a slow burn bop that takes a while to creep into your heart and lodge itself there. The angst is real though, with the delicate electronic backing track almost fading into the background as it low-key sets the mood. Vocals push through to make a pleading case that urges us to be honest because faking is heartbreaking.

## DNA (2017)

The song opens with summery strumming and breezy whistles signalling a more relaxed and confident BTS, and then it slams into an utter banger. Like many of the best BTS singles, *DNA* builds and builds with beats and tempos rising and falling before releasing with electronic violin squeals that play like a chorus. A crisp masterclass in keeping the ear interested.

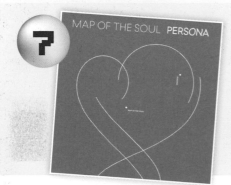

## DIONYSUS (2019)

The ode to the Greek God of wine and partying is a totally amped up rock/rap/pop crossover slayer that thrashes to the beat of a heavy metal drum. It's so frantically infectious, that had *Boy With Luv* not existed, it could have been the lead song from their *Map Of The Soul: Persona* EP. One of the most exciting things BTS have ever done.

# POSITION IMPOSSIBLE

**When K-Pop groups start out, each member is assigned their positions: check out the roles in BTS.**

**V**
- Sub-vocalist
- Visual
- Lead dancer

**SUGA**
- Lead rapper

**JIN**
- Sub-vocalist
- Visual

## ROLE CALL

**Main:** This person is considered the absolute best – given a lot to do.

**Lead:** The exceptionally talented second best artists who will often support the main performer.

**Sub:** These guys aren't given the most, but bring unique and special moments to a song.

**Visual:** Arguably the most handsome – and there will be arguments - LOL.

**Maknae:** The youngest.

**Centre:** Usually placed in the middle of the group.

**Leader:** Duh, the leader – and in this case the translator.

### JUNGKOOK
- Main vocalist
- Lead dancer
- Sub-rapper
- Maknae
- Centre

### RM
- Main rapper
- Leader

### JIMIN
- Lead dancer
- Lead vocalist

### J-HOPE
- Main dancer
- Lead rapper

## LINER NOTES

**Members with something in common are sometimes grouped together as 'liners' and are said to be part of a certain line. There's a whole bunch of them in BTS.**

**Rap line**
RM, Suga, J-Hope

**Vocal line**
Jungkook, Jimin,
Jin, V

**Dance line**
J-Hope, Jimin,
Jungkook, V

**Visual line**
Jin and V

**Maknae line** *(younger members)*
Jungkook, V, Jimin

**Hyung line** *(older members)*
Jin, Suga, J-Hope, RM

**Kim Line** *(all share the family name Kim)*
RM, V, Jin

**Busan Line** *(come from Busan)*
Jungkook, Jimin

**Daegu Line** *(come from Daegu)*
Suga, V

**95 line** *(born in 1995)*
Jimin, V

**94 line** *(born in 1994)*
J-Hope, RM

전정국

**Name:** Jeon Jungkook
**Born:** 1 September 1997
**Star sign:** Virgo (reliable, witty, perfectionist)
**From:** Busan, South Korea
**Height:** 5 feet 10 inches
**Defining features:** Scar on his cheeky face
**Usual position in group:** The centre

**LET'S MEET**

# JUNGKOOK

## If he was a Top Trump card he'd thrash everyone in the pack – 10, 10, 10s across the board!

JK auditioning at the tender age of 14.

### LUCKY SEVEN

When Jungkook auditioned for the talent show *Superstar K* in 2011, unbelievably he wasn't selected, but he wasn't sad for long. After the show aired he received seven offers from seven agencies desperate to sign him.

### GAMER

Jungkook is famously a fan of video games and admits that when he was younger he used to play them all the time! But now he's grown up and BTS is such a big part of his life, JK says he'd rather spend his free time doing things that make him a better person.

### 97 HEAVEN

Jungkook is a member of the infamous '97 Line' – that is K-Pop idols who were born in 1997. Other 97-Liners are SEVENTEEN's Min-gyu, DK and The8, Astro's Cha Eun-woo, NCT's Jae-hyun and BamBam Got7. They have a group chat and even meet up and hang out but will they record music together?

As the maknae of the band – ie: the youngest – Jungkook is supposed to be the cute one. Well, he is cute, but that's not all he does because, well, he does EVERYTHING except make the tea. He's the main singer, the lead dancer and a sub-rapper – all of which has earned him the title 'Golden Maknae'.

**GOLDEN BOY**

Jungkook masked his identity for a TV show.

### THE VOICE

He is the group's main vocalist because his voice is textbook brilliant. Even if you don't love BTS it's impossible to deny the pure clarity of his vocals on YouTube covers like Charlie Puth's *We Don't Talk Anymore* or his jaw-dropping appearance on the TV show *King of Masked Singer*.

# BOYZ WITH FUN

**BTS take themselves very seriously, except when they don't take themselves seriously at all!**

### "WHAAAAAT?"
Is Kim Taehyung the most expressive man in the world? He is a human tombola of emojis: crazy, happy, confused, shock, questioning? What's on his mind? If Jin doesn't know, then neither do we.

### ADVENTURE RECLINE
How does Jin sleep when BTS are on the road? Snuggled up to his Jake from Adventure Time travel pillow. The two are so close that Seokjin will wear the stretchy pup as a hat.

### RAY OF HOPE
J-Hope: I'm a very quiet, calm and thoughtful hyung. Also J-Hope: Wahhhhhhhhhh!!!!

## FLOWER BOYS
The face mask says don't look at me, the enormous sunflower head-garland tells a slightly different story.

J-Hope

Jin

Suga

## BUNNY HA-HA
'Halloween dance practice' – are there three sweeter words? Watching BTS goof around in ridiculous costumes is a delight, but Kookie as a bunny is a whole other level of perfection. JUST LOOK AT HIM.

...then there's Snow White and the Six Dwarves. Have you ever seen a more beautiful Disney Princess? Sorry Cinders, you're cancelled.

I can't breathe

## SKINSHIP
If we won an award, like Jimin, we'd take the chance to hug V really, really tightly.

# BEYOND THE SONGS

**We don't always understand what BTS are singing which is a pity because the lyrics are often very meaningful.**

● *Attack on Bangtan* is a reference to the Manga and Netflix anime show *Attack on Titan*, which BTS are big fans of.

● BTS reference Greek mythology in the song *Dionysus*. Dionysus was the god of wine, partying and earthly pleasure.

● Want a powerful message about female empowerment? Look no further than *21st Century Girl*.

Jin contemplates diving into space for the *Serendipity* MV.

● *Serendipity*, sung by Jimin, is believed to have been inspired by *The Little Prince* with its imagery of falling in love with a flower and space themes.

● An old school track BTS say they'd enjoy performing again is *Jump* – not V though, he hates it.

● The first K-Pop song Ed Sheeran ever wrote was *Make It Right* for BTS on *Map of the Soul: Persona*.

● *Go Go* from *Love Yourself: Her* explores modern day consumerism, and how we're often too focussed on money and what we can buy with it.

● *Spring Day* is a complex song but one of the inspirations behind it is the movie *Snowpiercer*, which is set in a wintery future where everyone lives on a train that never stops.

The MV for *Spring Day* features a journey through a train just like the *Snow Piercer* movie.

● Jungkook, Rap Monster and Taehyung all agree that their favourite BTS song to perform is *Save Me*.

● *Anpanman*, (on *Love Yourself: Tear*) is a massively popular Japanese cartoon character with a head made of bean-filled bread who has no real super powers. The message behind the song is obvious – you don't need to be big and strong and perfect to be super. Just be you.

● Are BTS fans of *RuPaul's Drag Race* season six winner Bianca Del Rio? Their song *Not Today*, which is a defiant anthem for the oppressed, is very similar to her catchphrase '*Not Today Satan*.'

**김석진**

**Name:** Kim Seok-jin
**Born:** 4 December 1992
**Star sign:** Sagittarius (curious, adventurous, friendly)
**From:** Gwacheon, Gyeonggi Province, South Korea
**Height:** 5 feet 10½ inches
**Defining features:** Full kissable lips: mwah!
**Usual position in group:** Third from left

## LET'S MEET

# JIN

## He was recently voted the idol people most wanted to have a picnic with, but what else is there to know?

### HI DAD

Jin may not be the leader, but he is the oldest member of BTS, and consequently is well known for making terrible 'dad jokes'. Adorbs.

Jin is everyone's favourite hyung (big brother).

Jin has the nickname Worldwide Handsome, which is fitting because he has the designated role of 'visual', which means he's the official eye-candy of BTS. Wonder what the rest of the band think? Hmmm?

CUTE

### YUM

If you ever go to Seoul, be sure to visit Jin's Japanese-inspired restaurant, Ossu Seiromushi in the Songpa district.

### SMARTY

In 2017 Jin graduated from Konkuk University with a bachelor's degree in acting and art, then he also enrolled at Hanyang Cyber University. Jin's graduation photo tweet had over 400,000 likes and over 180,000 retweets. Worldwide 'not just a pretty face' has a nice ring!

### VROOOOM!!!

Google: 'Car Door Guy' and Jin comes up. Why? Because when he was seen arriving at the 2015 Melon Music Awards the internet lost it. They didn't know who he was, just that he was a super cute guy opening a car door.

# RULE BREAKERS

To conform is the norm in South Korea, but BTS have become massive on their own terms.

## BTS IS LIFE: QUITE LITERALLY

Despite being one of the biggest bands on the planet, who could afford to buy a house anywhere in the world, BTS choose to live together in the same apartment complex: The Hill in Hannam, Seoul, proving BTS isn't just a job, but a way of life.

BTS are a force that can't be contained.

## THE OUTSIDERS

Big Hit, the entertainment company that look after BTS, is much smaller than K-pop mega-corps SM (EXO, Red Velvet) and JYP (TWICE, Stray Kids). This may have given them certain freedoms that groups coming from such a rigorous system don't enjoy, as well as making BTS the underdog, especially when they were just starting out.

## LYRICAL WARRIORS

Unlike many pop stars, BTS write much more than simple love songs – they've written about complex issues such as mental health, anxiety and depression, the education system, capitalism, feminism, and perhaps their most powerful message: self love, being true to yourself and not being a sheep.

## D.I.Y. NOT?

Many South Korean groups have a team of writers and producers that create all their hit songs – BTS have a team too, it's THEM. Writing and producing their own music means more work for the boys, but it gives them creative control, and also makes connecting with the music easier – because it comes straight from their hearts and laptops.

BTS do it all: they sing, they dance, they write and produce their material and make it all look effortless.

## OUTSPOKEN ARTISTS

The bigger an artist gets, the more they have to lose, which is why it's so inspiring to see BTS say what they feel about important issues, with the risk of alienating fans and sponsors alike. They say what they want with words and deeds: like the time they donated 100 million won (£68,000) to the survivors and families of the Sewol ferry disaster: a potentially rebellious act that may have seen them blacklisted by the government. ARMY appreciates this courage.

## LOW KEY ALLIES

BTS come from a country where in 2017 Amnesty International stepped in after a male soldier was sentenced to six months in prison for having a boyfriend, so supporting equality is a massive deal. RM championed Macklemore's gay anthem *Same Love*, Suga said: "Everyone is equal" and the band regularly endorse 'out' artists like Troye Sivan and Sam Smith.

Jungkook and RM recorded a cover of Troye Sivan's brilliant song *Fools* (pictured).

# 7 ESSENTIAL

# MUSIC VIDEOS
## TO WATCH

**BTS videos are almost as important as the songs – ACTION!**

## 1

### SPRING DAY
Is this the most beautiful BTS MV? For their epic ballad, the boys step out of the studio into the real world for a mini movie masterpiece, where everyone looks incredibly sad and unbearably pretty (Oh hai Jin) in the bleached out mists of late winter light. Stunning.

## 2

### DOPE
How to make a simple MV super-exciting: do it in a single take, while BTS pretend it's careers day. RM and Suga are military men, J-Hope is a racing driver, Jin a doctor, Jungkook a cop, Jimin is an office worker and lucky V is a sort of schoolboy scientist.

## 3

### FIRE
This is the video where BTS are going on a Hawaiian holiday, except they're not, they're going to a dark and dirty futuristic club where the bass is fat and someone keeps blowing up cars. There's fireworks, crowd surfing, and Jin is given a good ironing.

**4**

## BLOOD SWEAT & TEARS

From the moment Hobi lifts a delicate pair of opera glasses to his eyes we get an indication of what is about to follow: namely the most decadent and arty video BTS have ever made. Six mysterious mega minutes.

**5**

## MIC DROP

This Steve Aoki track features a darker side of BTS that recalls their early bad boy phase. A back to basics hip-hop MV that showcases agro choreo in bare studios, a prison and a carpark. Oh and a guy blew up a bunch of cars – again. Someone really should stop this hoodlum.

**6**

## IDOL

There is a time for minimalism and it's not in the MV for *Idol*. The boys chuck everything at this and it is EVERYTHING. A psychedelic daydream of green-screen jungles, Snapchat filters, pagodas, sunsets, rabbit moons, and Taehyung's v expressive face.

**7**

## BOY WITH LUV

Every time BTS come back they seem to get bigger, better and bolder. Their smash MV to *Boy With Luv* featuring Halsey was a feast for the senses – it was so pink and delicious it almost looked edible. The boys wore silky fuchsia pyjamas and full on lippy giving us so much life.

## 민윤기

**Name:** Min Yoon-gi

**Born:** 9 March 1993

**Star sign:** Pisces (creative, idealistic, sensitive)

**From:** Daegu Town, South Korea

**Height:** 5 feet 9 inches

**Defining features:** Super-pale complexion

**Usual position:** Second from left

**LET'S MEET**

# SUGA

## The swag master gives Jungkook a run for his 'golden' status. Is there anything he can't do?

### LET IT FLOW

Suga was trying to make it as a rapper called 'Gloss' in a group called D-Town before BTS, and he was so good that he became one of the main rappers in BTS. He also writes and produces many of the band's songs, as well as those by other artists. Suga is also such a terrific piano player (and humble – ha!). He once dubbed himself: *Chopin of the beat*.

Suga didn't get his name from a love of candy, but because he is quite pale and sweet like sugar. Also his basketball position at school was: Shooting Guard – Shoo Gua = Suga.

**SWEET**

### LAZY?

Whenever Suga has free time he doesn't do very much, which has earned him the nickname Motionless Min. He's so chilled out that his Facebook page even names his special skill as: 'lying down'.

### PANTS

Suga once admitted to not only stealing, but wearing, Jungkook's underwear, and he refused to give it back saying there were holes in it. Was he sorry? Nope, in fact he said he'd do it again. Poor Kookie.

### HONESTY

BTS are known for telling it like it is and Suga is no different. On his solo mixtape *Agust D* he bravely opens up about his struggles with depression, OCD and social anxiety.

Wave hello to BTS's resident deep thinker.

# BEYOND THE STAGE

**BTS make some incredible music and videos but watching them perform – well that's pure magic.**

● The *Red Bullet Tour* of 2014/15 was BTS's first world tour. The boys played to audiences of around 3,000 to 10,000 across Asia, Australia, America and South America, but Europe unfortunately didn't get a look in – hashtag sadface.

● Like most K-Pop groups, when BTS perform there is a specific time and place to sing along with the lyrics, and other times when it's best to be quiet.

● The 2017 *Wings Tour* was produced in 12 countries, selling out in record time at some venues.

● The most daring part of the *Love Yourself* concert was Jungkook flying over the audience singing *Euphoria*.

● 140,000 people paid to watch the V-Live stream of BTS's historic Wembley concert: more than saw the show live.

● Tickets to BTS 2019 shows at Wembley Stadium sold out in 90 minutes. That's 120,000 ARMYs across two nights in London alone. The tour was seen by over a million people across the world.

● The stage outfits for BTS 2019 tour were designed by super chic French fashion house, Dior. Menswear designer Kim Jones said he was inspired by their winning personalities.

● Son Sung-deuk is BTS's ridiculously talented choreographer and performance director. In some ways he's the secret eighth member of the band. You might want to join the 700,000 followers he currently has on Instagram.

● Jimin and Jin have both spoken about their desire to stay as healthy as possible so that they can continue to perform for as many fans as possible in the future.

# FASHION ICONS

Presentation is important to all K-groups, but BTS go above and beyond to totally slay the fashion game.

## SHIRTY

'Cold shoulder' tops are very popular with women of a certain age – and Korean boybands obviously.

## ARTY

If there's a gallery opening across town BTS are totally going. But what even is art?

## DRESSY

The perfect pop package tied up neatly with a bow ... tie.

## BLANKY

Jin wears granny's best blanket, while Suga rocks her tablecloth.

## FRILLY

If you call BTS: a bunch of big girls' blouses, they take it as a compliment and ask, 'Do you have it in a medium?'

### SKINNY

Back in 2016 cammo-cloud-tropical was a definite thing. Jin did not get the memo.

### GUCCI

Have you ever seen a more dapper bunch of boys? Pretty–preppy–spendy.

### SHINY

BTS are always nap-ready in these silky suits. Pyjamas as outerwear has to be the best trend ever.

김태형

**Name:** Kim Tae-hyung

**Born:** 30 December 1995

**Star sign:** Capricorn (mature, confident, driven)

**From:** Seo District, Daegu, South Korea

**Height:** 5 feet 10½ inches

**Defining features:** Beautiful expressive face

**Usual position:** Far left

# V

## He's not the main singer, dancer or rapper, he's next level awesome just being himself.

### SHETCHY

Taehyung loves to draw and often carries a sketchbook. He is a particular fan of 80s street artist and celebrated painter Jean-Michel Basquiat tweeting 'dreams come true' when he saw his works in Paris. V also customised clothes inspired by JMB.

### SNAPPY

We all like taking arty photos on our smart phones, but for V it's a lot more than that. He loves taking pictures and has even created a snappy alter-ego, Vante, a portmanteau of his name and acclaimed Australian photographer Ante Badzim. Badzim, who is known for his bleached out and beautiful minimalist images, has since reached out and suggested a collaboration.

### BEYOND THE SCENERY

V might seem a little more low-key than some BTS members but when he released his touching self-written ballad *Scenery*, it became the most streamed song by any solo BTS member, hitting 100 million streams in just 14 days. V, V impressive.

V is not the easiest name to Google, but maybe that's why TaeTae chose it. It stands for victory – something BTS know quite a lot about. Before

**VICTORY**

launching with BTS, V was thinking of using the names Lex or Six.

### I PURPLE YOU

BTS's resident artist created his own catchphrase. V explained that purple is the last colour of the rainbow, so when he says: 'I purple you,' it means I will trust and love you for a very long time.

### SAX SYMBOL

What do V and Lisa Simpson have in common? They're smart, they love jazz and they both play the saxophone.

# DANCE MOVES
## TO MASTER

**Singing along to BTS is hard. Dancing along? Just try and stop us!**

### ❶ BOY WITH LUV

If you learn one move to this song, it should be the jerky alternating robotic arms and leg kick during the "Oh-oh-oh-oh-oh" parts of the chorus, but feel free to pat your body down during the "Oh my my my" section or even attempt Jimin's boot-scootin' heel kicks.

### ❷ IDOL

When the chorus hits with the first set of "Oh-oh-oh-ohs" get ready to shimmy and shake your hand down by your hip as if you were trying to shake the last ketchup from the bottle, before shooting your arm into the air à la John Travolta's famous *Night Fever* move.

### ❸ FIRE

There's a lot going on in the dance routine for *Fire*, but the one move every ARMY needs to get down is the dancing on the spot move with incoming arms. Imagine you're stamping out an actual fire, or really need a wee, while your arms lift and extend like airplanes.

**4**

## BLOOD SWEAT & TEARS

BTS has some great moves in this MV, like Jimin's shoulder flick, but there is also a lot of eye covering: the most famous of which is the crotch-grab and hip thrust move – but maybe go for your belt rather than Hobi's full on version.

**5**

## SINGULARITY

The MV to V's solo track *Singularity* has over 100 million views. The best section of the amazing clip is at the start when Taehyung performs that classic mime routine where you put your arm through a coat and pretend to be someone else.

**6**

## NOT TODAY

There's some easy basics to follow in this tricky routine. When Yoongi tells you to throw your hands up, you do as he says. And when the first refrain "Not today" comes, cross one arm and extend the other, wagging a finger to indicate you're not having it.

**7**

## SAVE ME

While the chorus involves a lot of wide stance jumps, spins and leg kicks, the verses allow for a more fluid interpretive dance style. Channel Maddie Ziegler and freestyle it out by throwing your entire body into the rhythm of the song and you won't go wrong.

# ROLE MODELS

## Would the world be filled with a lot less stress, if we all behaved a little bit more like BTS?

### MESSAGE SENT

With so many young fans, BTS realise what they say is important and potentially impactful. Their repeated message to "Love Yourself" is something young people who can be insecure, and caught in a negative cycle of social comparison on Insta, can't hear enough.

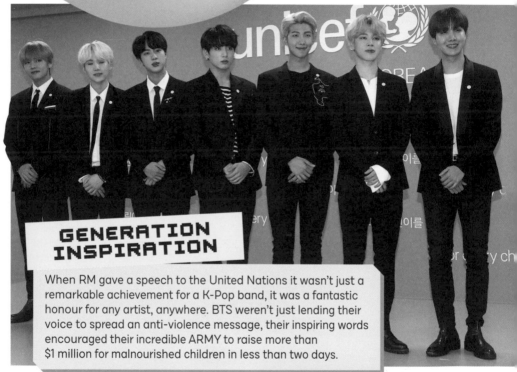

## GENERATION INSPIRATION

When RM gave a speech to the United Nations it wasn't just a remarkable achievement for a K-Pop band, it was a fantastic honour for any artist, anywhere. BTS weren't just lending their voice to spread an anti-violence message, their inspiring words encouraged their incredible ARMY to raise more than $1 million for malnourished children in less than two days.

Jin and V listen in to UN proceedings.

Namjoon gives his powerful speech to the UN.

LOVE YOURSELF 承 Her

> RM should stand for 'Role Model'

## GIVING BACK

BTS regularly donate to charities close to their hearts, donating much needed cash to pupils of their former schools, paying medical bills for their friends, helping out trainees, donating food to orphans, sending supplies to animal shelters, not to mention the funds they give to UNICEF from sales of their *Love Yourself* album.

## LIVE CLEAN

BTS may have courted a bad boy image at times, but despite their massive success they are never seen stumbling out of clubs, swearing, or acting in any way that could be seen as scandalous. Any controversies they encountered arose unintentionally and by accident rather than purposefully in poor taste.

## THEY CAME TO WERK!!!

Mums and dads across the world must be overjoyed with their children falling under the hard-working spell of BTS. They erase all ideas of millennials and gen-zers being lazy and wanting everything handed to them. Their schedule of touring, writing, recording, rehearsing, touring and performing is NON. STOP. No one works harder.

## DETOXIFYING MASCULINITY

BTS aren't afraid to experiment with their looks and are anything but predictable when it comes to making a fashion statement. Wearing make-up, dyeing their hair and rocking gender-challenging fashions you're unlikely to see down the high street: they've done it all.

Stunning in more ways than one. BTS serve up a smokey eye, nude lip and your mum's best scarf, in the MV for *Blood Sweat & Tears*.

# BEYOND THE SOCIALS

**Fans can connect instantly with BTS through their award-winning social media.**

● BTS have one important Twitter rule: No one can post after they've had a drink.

● BTS acknowledge their success is in part due to social media, but RM has stressed that their skills as musicians, performers and songwriters of sincerity should not be underestimated.

● BTS do not have individual social accounts, because they are ONE team.

● BTS have a bunch of associated Twitter accounts. They have over 20 million followers on @BTS_twt. @BTS_bighit has 15+ million followers, their Japanese account has 5+ million and their page for the adorable BT21 has 4+ million followers, while Big Hit Entertainment has 10+ million.

● At the time of writing, BTS's most popular Instagram pic has 4+ million likes.

● The most retweeted Twitter post of 2018 in South Korea was Jungkook singing a cover of *All My Life* by Park Won. It got 610,000 retweets snatching a Golden Tweet award.

● BTS aren't just popular on social media – they hold the Guinness world record for most Twitter engagements of anyone ever. The boys average 330,624 interactions per post.

● The Billboard Music award for Top Social Artist has been won by BTS three years in a row – and counting.

● At 14+ million followers BTS are easily the most followed artist on live streaming app V Live.

● *Boy With Luv* had the most YouTube views in 24 hours (74 million), beating BLACKPINK's *Kill this Love*, (56 million).

## 박지민

**Name:** Park Ji-min

**Born:** 13 October 1995

**Star sign:** Pisces (artistic, stylish, fair)

**From:** Busan, South Korea

**Height:** 5 feet 9 inches

**Defining features:** His abs and, ahem, his butt

**Usual position:** Second from right

# JIMIN

## The hard-working acrobatic firecracker of BTS proves that great things come in small packages.

Jimin is not only one of the best dancers in BTS, he is one of the best dancers in all of K-Pop. He studied contemporary dance growing up and is basically next level amazing.

**MOVER**

### NUMBER 1

South Korea loves a statistic and are constantly ranking K-Pop idols, which is as fascinating as it is brutal. Luckily for Jimin he regularly tops the Brand Reputation chart.

Jimin (BTS)
**PROMISE**

### FIGHTER

Thanks to a childhood love of the anime *One Piece*, and specifically the character Zoro, Jimin trained in Japanese martial arts for eight years.

**Jimin sadly missed Graham Norton's show.**

### OWWWCH!

Jimin is such a perfectionist that he is liable to suffer from occasional injury. When BTS came over to the UK, Jimin couldn't appear on *The Graham Norton Show* due to severe muscle pain in his neck and back. Take it easy, Jiminie.

It took Jimin months to write his first song *Promise*, but with some encouragement from RM he ended up releasing an uplifting song of encouragement. It was streamed 8.5 million times in 24 hours on SoundCloud – the most ever on the music platform.

### JIBOOTY

Fans are so appreciative of Jimin's peachy bum that they named it the Jibooty. He can even break chopsticks with his buttocks. #GOALS.

**The War of Hormone MV slaps serious butt!**

# BOYZ WITH LUV

## BTS are fully-grown men and really shouldn't be this frickin' adorable – check the evidence.

### DOGGY DAYCARE
Most of us like to cuddle puppies, but Jimin knows that dogs are people too. Instead of just stroking this little guy, ChimChim took the pup to the window to watch the world go by.

### GRATEFUL ... DEAD!
Back in 2016 BTS won their first best album award at the Melon Music Awards and totally lost it. Watching them fight back tears of joy and pride showed us how humble, genuine and wonderful they are.

### BTZZZZZ
It's probably fair to say that BTS are permanently zonked. They travel so much, that they grab 40 winks wherever they spot a spare sofa. Not sure why watching them sleep is so satisfying, but damn they're cute.

HBA HBA

### SURPRISE KING OF AEGYO
When BTS took part in a televised aegyo battle, of course J-Hope was going to win: he puts the aww into adawwwbs, but the big surprise was Suga. Looks like someone really does have a sweet side.

### BIG BOYS DO CRY

Dolly Parton is an icon and proved her power when she brought Jungkook to tears during her 2019 performance at the Grammys. Kookie is award show gold: he snacks, he cries, he dances in his seat.

### FETUS FEELS

One of BTS's earliest uploads is also one of the cutest: a video of Jimin, JK and Hobi performing *Graduation Song* in school uniforms looking like children, which they basically were – Jungkook was a fresh-faced 15.

### FLY BOYS

The law dictates that if you have an album called *Wings*, you absolutely must pretend to be a little bird and flap your tiny pretend wings: "Chirp. Cheep. Tweet."

# RECORD BREAKERS

**BTS break records with every release and frankly it's impossible to keep up.**

## BOY WITH LUV

● Most Viewed YouTube video/Music video/K-Pop video in 24 hours, with 74.6 million views.

● Most streamed song by a K-Pop group, with 29.9 million streams in one week.

**BTS are the only Korean artists to play Wembley stadium.**

BTS were the first K-Pop group to perform on American TV – at the American Music Awards in 2017 – pictured.

## BTS WORLD TOUR: LOVE YOURSELF IN SEOUL

● The biggest worldwide one-day box office for a cinema event. On 26 Jan 2019 the screening earned $11.7 million. The film was also the largest worldwide cinema event, playing in 4,100 cinemas in 102 territories.

## LOVE YOURSELF: TEAR
● The first Korean album to top the US album chart.

## WINGS
● The first album by a Korean artist to enter the UK album chart: at no 62.

## IDOL
● The first song by a Korean group to enter the UK top 40, reaching 21.

## DNA
● The first K-Pop group MV to hit a massive 350 million views.

## SPOTIFY
● The first group from Asia to reach 5 billion streams.

Jungkook knows where to look!

BTS are the first band since the Beatles to have three chart-topping albums in America in less than a year.

## MAP OF THE SOUL: PERSONA
● The best-selling album ever in South Korea, sold 3,229,032 copies in its first month, more than any other, beating the 1995 record of Kim Gun-mo's album *Mis-Encounter*.
● The first K-Pop album to get to number one in the UK.
● The most pre-orders for an album in South Korea at 2.6 million.

## TWITTER
● Most Twitter engagements ever, scoring 422,228 as of 29 April 2019, besting Harry Styles' record: 115,559.
● The first Korean Twitter account to hit 20 million followers.
● BTS were the most tweeted about celebrities in 2017, more than Donald Trump and Justin Bieber combined.

# BEYOND THE STYLE

**K-Pop is about the complete package, so of course fashion is incredibly important to the boys of BTS.**

● Jungkook describes his unfussy style of dressing as 'clean cut'.

● Looking good is important for Suga but he thinks it's important for clothes to be comfortable.

● RM thinks the clothes you wear reflect who you are as a person before you even say a word. He is fan of Japanese brands Neighbourhood and WTAPS.

● Jin is all about keeping it simple, but that doesn't mean he doesn't get it wrong, confessing that his worst fashion fail was wearing a totally pink outfit: top and trousers. Sounds fly to us!

● V takes style inspiration from old movies, and says fashion is one of the most important things in his life. Some of his favourite designers are: Gucci, Burberry, Saint Laurent and Vetements.

● J-Hope believes that clothes are important to BTS because they influence how the band feels, especially when they're performing.

● Jimin says that he never really thought about fashion till after BTS debuted.

● Kanye West is a major style influence for RM and Suga, but Jungkook rates the styling in BTS's very own *Dope* MV.

● When it comes to skincare, most of the boys swear by sheet masks, toner and moisturiser. RM's fave face care brand is Mediheal.

● Jungkook has never had long hair, but he wants to grow it one day. Do it, JK!

● Whenever they come to London, BTS go shopping at Liberty and London's posh shopping street Saville Row.

정호석

**Name:** Jung Ho-seok
**Born:** 18 February 1994
**Star sign:** Aquarius (analytical, original, independent)
**From:** Gwangju, South Korea
**Height:** 5 feet 10 inches
**Defining features:** His cheekbones and his smile
**Usual position:** Far right

# J-HOPE

## The sunshine of BTS is a BTS triple threat – he dances, he raps, and gives really great aegyo.

### NOPE TO HOPE

BTS have said that before J-Hope came up with his stage name he wasn't that hopeful, but somehow the name inspired him to live with more hope and happiness than before. Now Hoseok is the life and soul of the party.

### EAR EAR

J-Hope is the only member of BTS not to have his ears pierced. After he was spotted wearing earrings on V Live he cleared up the misunderstanding telling fans that they were only ear cuffs.

### JYPED

J-Hope auditioned for entertainment company JYP and if he'd got in might have gone on to join 2PM or Got7, but he didn't make it and JYP's loss was Big Hit's gain. J-Hope is an essential member of BTS who has helped to write most of BTS's biggest hits from *Blood Sweat & Tears* to *Boy With Luv*.

**DANCER**

Even before BTS, J-Hope was killing it with the dance moves. He went to the same dance academy as Big Bang's Seungri, 2NE1's Minzy and B.A.P's Zelo, and won a South Korea dance competition, which instantly woke everyone in the industry up to his talents.

### SCHOLARSHIP

J-Hope is not just rolling in banknotes, now he's successful, he's sharing the wealth and in May 2019 donated 100 million won (approx. £65,000) for scholarships at a girls' school. This was no one off, Hobi regularly gives money to children from low-income families.

**A ceremony for 10 girls of Jeonnam Girls' School who will receive five-year scholarships.**

# 7 ESSENTIAL

# YOUTUBE CLIPS

## TO STREAM

### BOY WITH LUV PERFORMANCE ON SNL

The MV to *Boy With Luv* is maje eye candy, but the intimate *SNL* performance sees the boys perform the entire choreography of the song while singing live and needs to be seen.

### BUZZFEED INTERVIEW WITH PUPPIES

It's very hard to pay attention to the questions in this filmed chat because the boys have been handed puppies and looking at them, looking at them is too much heaven. *Newsnight* take note.

### FLINCH

James Corden has a segment on his chat show where he fires projectiles at guests, while they stand behind a protective screen. The aim is to see if you can resist flinching. Watch BTS jump out of their skin - except V who is a literal statue.

### ROOKIE KING: CHANNEL BANGTAN EPISODE 4

In the 2013 variety show from SBS MTV, J-Hope is given the dare to kiss V. So he does what any man would do in such a situation: puts on some flaming red lipstick and gives him a big smacker – mwah!

RIDE THE PONY

### JIMMY FALLON'S FORTNITE DANCE CHALLENGE

BTS take it in turns to dance a random dance as executed by the charatcters of online video game *Fortnite*. V doing the Charleston is entertainment excellence as is RM's Ride The Pony with its serious Psy feels.

I've been your friend for seven years...

### THE NOISEY QUESTIONNAIRE OF LIFE

When Jin confesses to the interviewer that he has no friends, your heart might die a little. But his BTS brothers aren't sad for Jin, they're hurt, insisting that *they* are his friends. It's all too much.

### WEEKLY IDOL GIRL GROUP COVER DANCE

Watching BTS interpret some of K-Pop's biggest girl groups is what the internet was made for. Jungkook getting down to EXID's *Up and Down* is eye-watering brilliance. V's attempt at *Gee* by SNSD is also life.

# BOYZ WITH MERCH

**There is so much amazing BTS merchandise that we're going to need second jobs to pay for it all.**

## BACKPACKS

Take your stanning to school, work, the park, EVERYWHERE – because frankly people need constant BTS reminders.

## TRAINERS

BTS x Puma have to be the first trainer to encourage you to stop doing sport and put your feet up: otherwise how will people see your dope soles?

## DOLLS

Bye, bye Ken, Barbie has a new boyfriend, well seven of them to be honest. Mattel have created their own line of BTS dolls with replica outfits from the *Idol* M/V, and suddenly we're getting Barbie's Dream House out of the attic for them to live in. If the Mattel dolls are not cute enough you can always buy a BTS Be@rbrick, or collect the beyond-cute Funko Pop! Dolls.

## BT21 LINE FRIENDS

VAN THE SPACE ROBOT PROTECTS BT21 AND REPRESENTS ARMY

MANG (J-HOPE)

COOKY (JUNGKOOK)

SHOOKY (SUGA)

TATA (V)

CHIMMY (JIMIN)

KOYA (RM)

RJ (JIN)

When BTS teamed up with Asian mobile giant Line they didn't just smile and take the money, they sat down and helped design a new range of characters called BT21 (BTS + 21st Century) – the cuties are a team of 8 wannabe K-Pop idols each designed and representing each of BTS, and the eighth is ARMY. Yay. The characters have enjoyed crossovers with Converse and Hello Kitty and frankly we love them almost as much as the boys themselves.

## LEGO

Will we see BTS in the next Lego Movie? It's possible. The super seven are brick ready and even have their own stage.

## MAKE-UP

In South Korea make-up is massive business, even for boys, so of course BTS with their flawless-looking skin released a line with Korean Cosmetics company VT.

## COCA-COLA

Sorry Fanta, you're over. If a fizzy beverage doesn't have Jungkook's face on it, we're not drinking it.

# BULLET POINT BOY SCOUTS

**Before you go, please direct your eyes to some more important Bangtan bits you need to know.**

● According to Jin, their managers, Big Hit, devote 2/3 of their time to work and leave 1/3 for free time.

**Work. Eat. Rest. Repeat.**

● In 2018 BTS extended their contract with Big Hit until 2026. How old will we be then?

● When it comes to English, J-Hope finds it hard to say the word 'appreciate', V can't say 'singularity' and Jungkook is frustrated by the word 'frustrated'.

● Rapmon isn't the only BTS translator, BTS's long-time official translator is a man called John.

**RM's looking cute and feline fine in the MV to Idol.**

● Namjoon is the only 'cat person' in BTS. Everyone else loves dogs.

● Jungkook is the best at putting on make-up and the worst at replying to texts.

● The band like to eat bananas before a show to give them energy.

● Jimin bumped into Shawn Mendes in the loo at The Grammy's and didn't know if he should say hello, but luckily Shawn recognised him and said "Hi!" first.

● The BTS travelling entourage consists of over 30 people and includes managers, groomers, drivers, photographers, guards, interpreters, a choreographer and a masseur.

● When BTS go to the movies they always go to the first or last showing of the day – so it's super quiet and no one will see them. Sneaky.

**Movie nights, as seen in the *Lights* MV, are a proper giggle.**

● BTS have said that they think V is the best rapper in the vocal unit and that Suga is the best singer in the rap unit.

● The unofficial colour of BTS is purple. When BTS were in New York they lit the Empire State Building purple. Why? Because New York 'purples' BTS.

● BTS are inspired by writers such as Murakami, Camus and Herman Hesse.

● The boys have had many different hair colours but V and J-Hope's favourite was red, RM prefers silver, Jin: pink, while Jungkook and Suga like it black and easygoing Jimin loves them all.

# CREDITS

**Front cover:** PICTURES: Image Press Agency / Alamy Images, Top Photo Corporation / Alamy Images, Newscom / Alamy Images, Hyperstar / Alamy Images, ZUMA Press, Inc. / Alamy Images.
**4-5:** PICTURES: ZUMA Press, Inc. / Alamy Images.
**6-7:** PICTURES: Everett Collection Inc / Alamy Images, ZUMA Press, Inc. / Alamy Images, Erik Pendzich / Alamy Images, MediaPunch Inc / Alamy Images.
**8-9:** WORDS: Koreaboo.com, Wikepedia.com. PICTURES: Newscom / Alamy Images, TopPhoto/Alamy Live News, Big Hit Entertainment.
**10-11:** WORDS: Wikipedia.com, Yonhap news agency, Yibada.com. PICTURES: Aflo Co. Ltd. / Alamy Images, Top Photo Corporation /Alamy Images, Big Hit Entertainment.
**12-13:** WORDS: Officialcharts.com, cnet.com: Katie Conner. PICTURES: Top Photo Corporation /Alamy Images, Newscom / Alamy Images, Big Hit Entertainment.
**14-15:** WORDS: Koreaboo.com, Billboard.com: Tamar Herman, Soompi.com: DeeDeeGii. PICTURES: Image Press Agency / Alamy Images.
**16-17:** WORDS: Koreaboo.com, Billboard.com; Xander Zellener. PICTURES: Top Photo Corporation / Alamy Images, Newscom / Alamy Images, YONHAPNEWS AGENCY via Mnet, tvN
**18-19:** PICTURES: Big Hit Entertainment.
**20-21:** WORDS: Koreaboo.com, kprofiles.com. PICTURES: ZUMA Press, Inc. / Alamy Images.
**22-23:** WORDS: Koreaboo.com. PICTURES: Top Photo Corporation / Alamy Images, Newscom / Alamy Images, YONHAPNEWS AGENCY via King of Masked singer: Munhwa Broadcasting Corporation.
**24-25:** PICTURES: ZUMA Press, Inc. / Alamy Images, Top Photo Corporation / Alamy Images, Newscom / Alamy Images, YouTube/ Bangtan Bomb: Big Hit Entertainment.
**26-27:** WORDS: Ask Anything Chat/ iHeartMedia, inc, Soompi: S.Park. PICTURES: Newscom / Alamy Images, Malcolm Fairman / Alamy Images, The Photo Access / Alamy Images, Big Hit Entertainment, Attack on Titan: Netflix/ Wit studio, Inc, Pony studio, Inc.
**28-29:** WORDS: Koreaboo.com, SBS.com.au, Culturetrip.com, Mimsie Ladner, Wikipedia.com. PICTURES: Top Photo Corporation /Alamy Images, Newscom / Alamy Images, Melon Music Awards, Kakao M.
**30-31:** WORDS: Billboard.com: E. Alex Jung , Soompi.com, New York Times: Chloe Sang Hun, Metro.co.uk: Alicia Adejobi. PICTURES: Image Press Agency / Alamy Images, Aflo Co. Ltd. / Alamy Images, EMI Australia/Capitol Records.
**32-33:** PICTURES: Big Hit Entertainment.
**34-35:** WORDS: Koreaherald.com, Soompi.com, Koreaboo.com, Cuvism Magazine, Metro.co.uk: Amy Duncan. PICTURES: Top Photo Corporation / Alamy Images, Newscom / Alamy Images, Geisler-Fotopress GmbH /Alamy Images, Big Hit Entertainment.
**36-37:** WORDS: NME.com: Elizabeth Aubrey, GQ-magazine.co.uk: Faye Fearon, Kpopmap.com, Wikipedia.com, Metro.co.uk: Sarah Deen, Tobi Akingbade, soompi.com: J.K. PICTURES: Newscom / Alamy Images.
**38-39:** PICTURES: Aflo Co. Ltd. / Alamy Images, Top Photo Corporation / Alamy Images, Rebecca Tsien / Alamy Images, Newscom / Alamy Images, Image Press Agency / Alamy Images, UPI /Alamy Images.
**40-41:** WORDS: Koreaboo.com, Soompi.com, Hellokpop.com: Yann Magcamit, Boredpanda.com: Vaiva Vareikaite. PICTURES: Newscom / Alamy Images, Top Photo Corporation / Alamy Images, Stephen Chung / Alamy Images, YONHAPNEWS AGENCY via Star Show 360: Munhwa Broadcasting Corporation.
**42-43:** PICTURES: Big Hit Entertainment.
**44-45:** WORDS: Rolling Stone: Jae Ha Kim, Independent: Clémence Michallon, Koreaboo.com. PICTURES: Newscom / Alamy Images, UPI /Alamy Images, Big Hit Entertainment.
**46-47:** WORDS: Twitter/ BTS/ Big Hit Entertainment, Koreahcrald.com: Yonhap, Instagram, Guinessworldrecords.com, eonline.com: Hanan Haddad, Billboard.com: Tamar Herman. PICTURES: Newscom / Alamy Images.
**48-49:** WORDS: Billboard.com: Tamar Herman, Forbes.com: Tamar Herman, Kstarlive.com, Metro.co.uk: Adam Starkey, Soompi.com: E.Cha, Popcrush.com. PICTURES: Newscom / Alamy Images, Top Photo Corporation / Alamy Images, The Graham Norton Show: BBC, Big Hit Entertainment.
**50-51:** PICTURES: Top Photo Corporation / Alamy Images, Grammy Awards/ Big Hit Entertainment, Idol Party/ Chosun Broadcasting Company, Melon Music Awards/ Kakao M, YouTube.com.
**52-53:** WORDS: Billboard.com: Tamar Herman, Kevin Rutherford, Guinness World Records, Cosmo.ph: Lily Grace Tabanera, Metro.co.uk: Louise Griffin, Forbes.com: Caitlin Kelley, SBS.com.au, Iheart.com: Rose Whythe. PICTURES: Everett Collection Inc / Alamy Images.
**54-55:** WORDS: Allure.com: Devon Abeleman, Pastemagazine.com : Mathias Rosenzweig and Mitchell Harrison, Vogue.co.uk: Naomi Pike, Koreaboo.com. PICTURES: Top Photo Corporation / Alamy Images.
**56-57:** WORDS: Allkpop.com, Koreaboo.com, Koreaherald.com: Lee So-jeong, NME.com: Elizabeth Aubrey. PICTURES: Top Photo Corporation / Alamy Images, PictureLux / The Hollywood Archive / Alamy Images, Jeonnam Girls' Commercial High School, VLive: Big Hit Entertainment.
**58-59:** PICTURES: YouTube/Saturday Night Live: NBC Televison, YouTube/Buzzfeed, YouTube /The Late, Late Show with James Cordon: CBS Television, YouTube/ Rookie King: Channel Bangtan, YouTube/ SBS MTV, YouTube/ The Tonight Show starring Jimmy Fallon: NBC Television, YouTube/ Noisey: Vice media LLC, YouTube/ Weekly Idol: Genie Pictures/ MBC Plus.
**60-61:** PICTURES: BTSmania.com/ Big Hit Entertainment, Mattel Inc, The Coca-Cola Company, Puma SE, Funko Inc, The Lego Group, VT Cosmetics, Line Corporation.
**62-63:** WORDS: Forbes.com: Tamar Herman, Soompi.com: JK, EW.com: Leah Greenblatt, Rolling Stone.com: Chris Martins, Buzzfeed.com: Elaina, Wahl, Sarah Han. PICTURES: Newscom / Alamy Images, Design Pics Inc / Alamy Images, LANDMARK MEDIA / Alamy Images.
**64:** PICTURES: Bruce Cotler/Globe Photos via ZUMA Wire, Alamy Stock Photo.
**Back cover:** PICTURES: ZUMA Press, Inc. / Alamy Images.